INTRODUCTION

"Why don't you write stories for children?" I don't know how many times well meaning friends have said this to me. I suppose that — knowing that I am a journalist — they assume that I should find it easier to write for children than for anybody else. But experience has taught me how very difficult it is for a writer to enter that special world, half reality, half fantasy, in which children live and dream.

So I had a better idea. I let my six-year-old daughter make up stories for herself. And I put them down on paper. I hope you like them as much as I do.

S.A. Hughes.

This edition published 1979 by
Sackett & Marshall Ltd
2 Great Marlborough St, London W1
Produced by Sackett Publicare Ltd
2 Great Marlborough St, London W1

ISBN 0 86109 046 2

Filmset by TypeMatters (London) Ltd, London
Printed in Italy by New Interlitho SpA

CONTENTS

The Apple that Nobody Wanted

Once there was a apple which had the longest stalk in the world. It was as long as a bus. It was so long that nobody wanted to eat it, which is not a good thing if you are a apple.

One day a alligator came along and he said: "Oh, I think I can manage that apple!" And he gobbled it all up, right down to the last pip.

Sometimes I think this is rather a sad sort of story.

Omar the Goose

Omar the Goose went out to wander over a fardly plain. He had been sitting in the same spot for so long that it was a great treat to wander, and he did enjoy himself. He was a charming goose. The only trouble was that he was always slimming and eating. He couldn't stop eating and he couldn't stop slimming. It seems a dreadful shame. Especially such a charming goose.

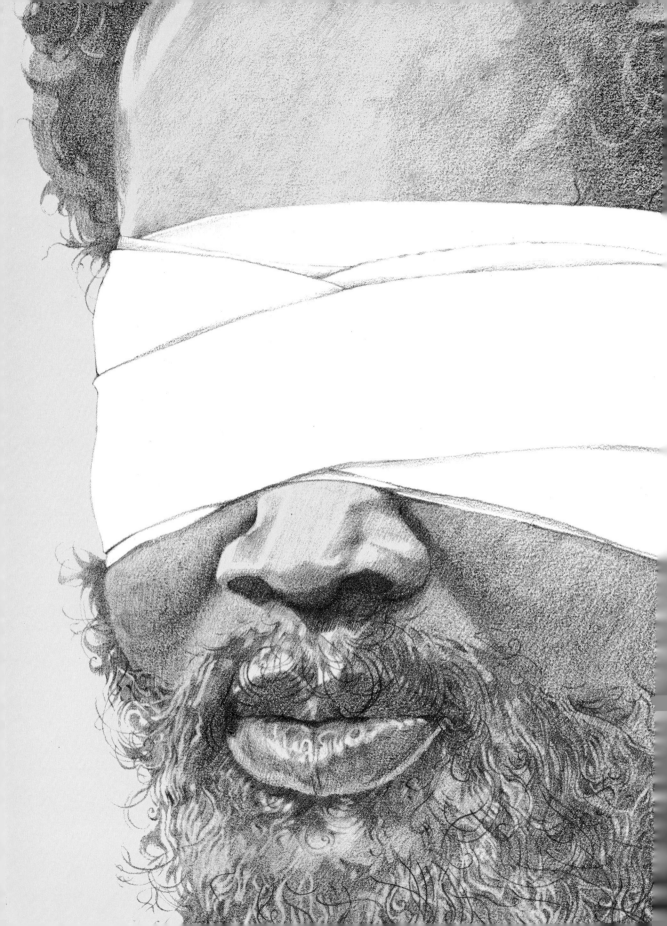

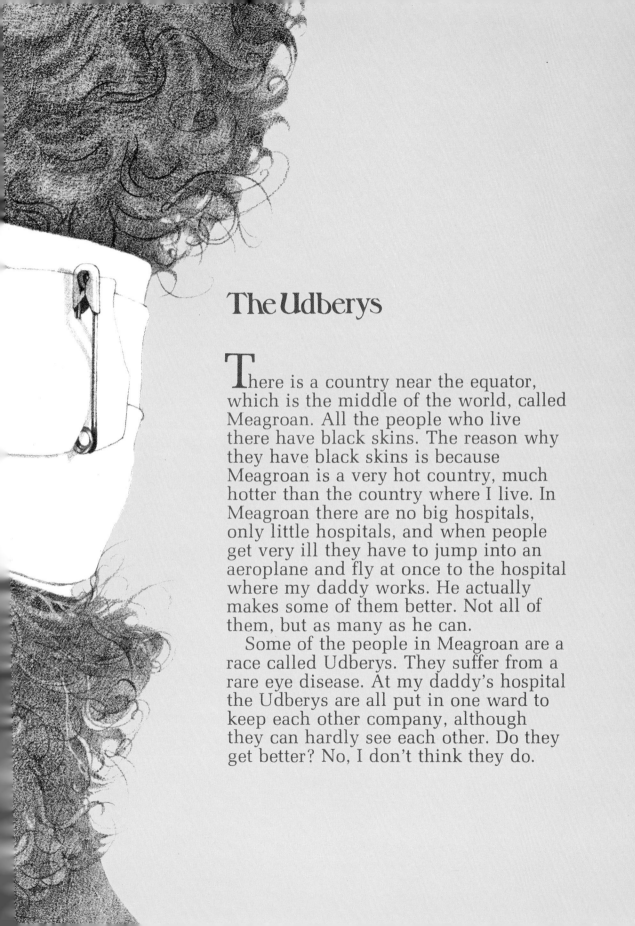

The Udberys

There is a country near the equator, which is the middle of the world, called Meagroan. All the people who live there have black skins. The reason why they have black skins is because Meagroan is a very hot country, much hotter than the country where I live. In Meagroan there are no big hospitals, only little hospitals, and when people get very ill they have to jump into an aeroplane and fly at once to the hospital where my daddy works. He actually makes some of them better. Not all of them, but as many as he can.

Some of the people in Meagroan are a race called Udberys. They suffer from a rare eye disease. At my daddy's hospital the Udberys are all put in one ward to keep each other company, although they can hardly see each other. Do they get better? No, I don't think they do.

The Two Wellingtons

Once there was two wellingtons called Charles and Miston. They lived in a cardboard box behind the back door. One day Charles said to Miston: "Let's go out and find some water and play in it." "All right," said Miston. So off they plodded.

They had a lot of mud on them and it wasn't easy to get going, but eventually they came to a farm with chickens and goats and all sorts of exciting things. But suddenly they heard a something in the sky. It was a helicopter. It seemed awfully low. "Oh dear," said Miston, "I'm not used to this sort of a thing. Let's go back." So they ran back to the house as fast as they could go and jumped into their box behind the back door.

The Biscuit who Laughed

One day I heard an awful rattle in the
biscuit tin and when I opened the lid,
which I'm not supposed to do, one of
the biscuits leapt right out and danced
all round the kitchen, and off the table
and onto the kitchen floor. He laughed
and laughed, and in the end he laughed
himself all into pieces and ended up
horrid crumbs all over the kitchen floor.
Which was a pity, as he was my
favourite kind of biscuit.

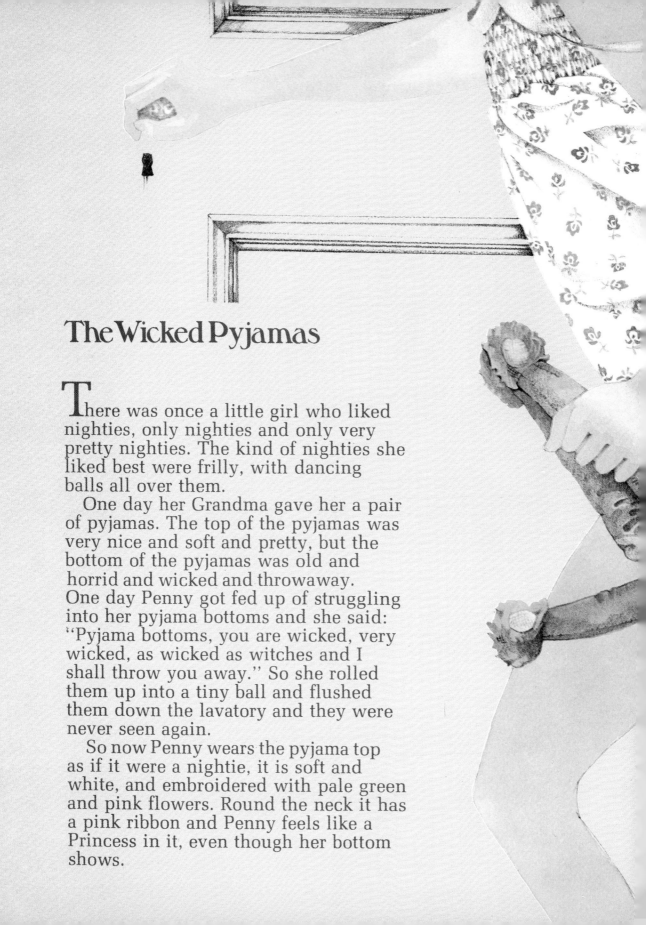

The Wicked Pyjamas

There was once a little girl who liked nighties, only nighties and only very pretty nighties. The kind of nighties she liked best were frilly, with dancing balls all over them.

One day her Grandma gave her a pair of pyjamas. The top of the pyjamas was very nice and soft and pretty, but the bottom of the pyjamas was old and horrid and wicked and throwaway. One day Penny got fed up of struggling into her pyjama bottoms and she said: "Pyjama bottoms, you are wicked, very wicked, as wicked as witches and I shall throw you away." So she rolled them up into a tiny ball and flushed them down the lavatory and they were never seen again.

So now Penny wears the pyjama top as if it were a nightie, it is soft and white, and embroidered with pale green and pink flowers. Round the neck it has a pink ribbon and Penny feels like a Princess in it, even though her bottom shows.

The Qualacin

The qualacin is very rare. It is rare in London and rare all over England. So you hardly ever see it, but should you happen to see it, it is always red. Red all over, bright red, even its eyes. So if you ever see anything that looks like that, that's what it is.

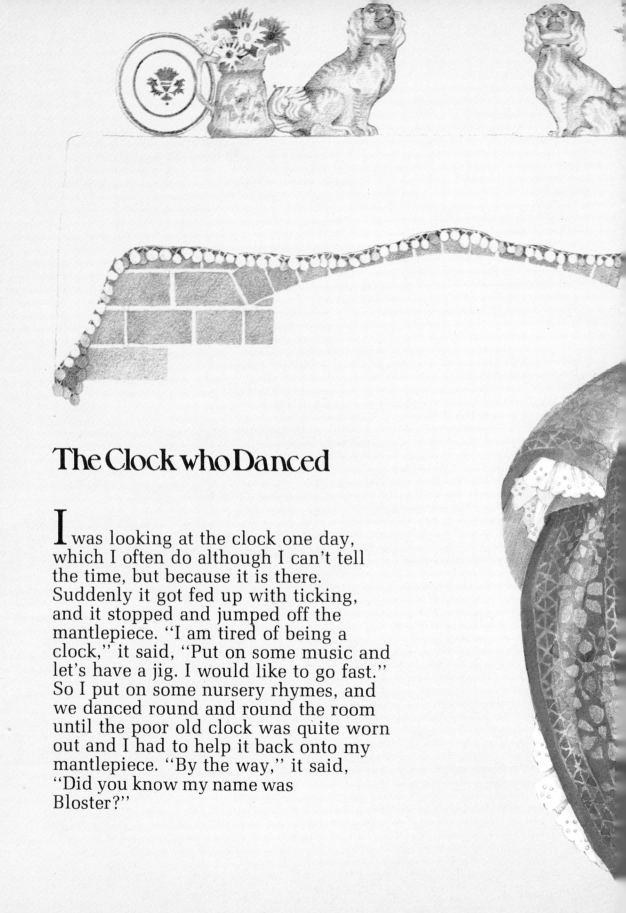

The Clock who Danced

I was looking at the clock one day, which I often do although I can't tell the time, but because it is there. Suddenly it got fed up with ticking, and it stopped and jumped off the mantlepiece. "I am tired of being a clock," it said, "Put on some music and let's have a jig. I would like to go fast." So I put on some nursery rhymes, and we danced round and round the room until the poor old clock was quite worn out and I had to help it back onto my mantlepiece. "By the way," it said, "Did you know my name was Bloster?"

Kelligant Pig

Once there was a pig called Kelligant
Pig. He was a tame pig, not a wild boar
or anything like that, and he lived in
the kitchen like a dog.
The place he liked to sit best was on a
box of chocolates, a big box of
Christmas chocolates which hadn't even
been given to him but to someone else
in the family, a child probably. And
now no-one likes to eat those Christmas
chocolates because Kelligant Pig has sat
on them so long. I daresay they would
be all right, because he hasn't gone
through the lid, but somehow nobody
fancies them.

The Gospits

Have you heard about the Gospits?
They are very small people, elves
probably, and they live inside leaves.
One evening I crept into the garden and
I heard one coughing and choking
inside his leaf. I suspect he was having
a dream. Or perhaps he was trying to
think who he was. A Gospit must
worry about that sometimes.

The Magic Crabs

Once there was a little girl called Penny and she went to a beach, the biggest and sandiest in the world, and she digged and digged until she found a jar full of crabs. She took them to her home and left them outside the back door. But in the morning, do you know? An awful thing. All the crabs had disappeared. Maybe they had gone away by a fairy. Or another thing. Maybe they had made their own way back to the beach.

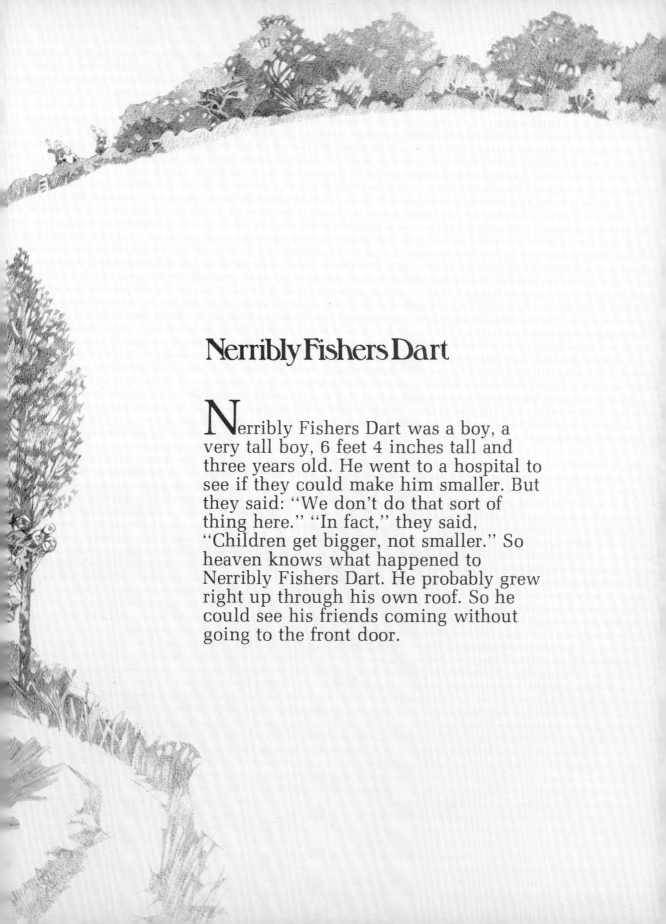

Nerribly Fishers Dart

Nerribly Fishers Dart was a boy, a very tall boy, 6 feet 4 inches tall and three years old. He went to a hospital to see if they could make him smaller. But they said: "We don't do that sort of thing here." "In fact," they said, "Children get bigger, not smaller." So heaven knows what happened to Nerribly Fishers Dart. He probably grew right up through his own roof. So he could see his friends coming without going to the front door.

The Christmas Story

This is the story of the Birth of Jesus. Do you know the story of the Birth of Jesus? No? Well then, I'll start. He lived a long time ago. In the 19th century. I think. One night some shepherds were watching over their flocks. They saw a light in the sky. It must be lightning they thought, but no, it was an Angel. "Hello," he said, "Would you like to see the Birth of Jesus?" "Yes, thanks very much," they replied. "It's in a stable," said the Angel, "In a distant country." "All right," said the head sheep man, "Let's follow him." And off they went. Then the clock struck twelve and the angel disappeared.

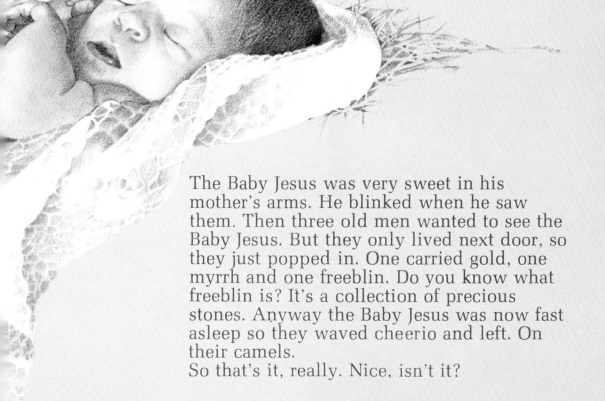

The Baby Jesus was very sweet in his mother's arms. He blinked when he saw them. Then three old men wanted to see the Baby Jesus. But they only lived next door, so they just popped in. One carried gold, one myrrh and one freeblin. Do you know what freeblin is? It's a collection of precious stones. Anyway the Baby Jesus was now fast asleep so they waved cheerio and left. On their camels.

So that's it, really. Nice, isn't it?

The Norfolk Divers

There are some people called The Norfolk Divers. They are not human people. They have human skin but it is a sort of grey. They have snappy jaws and big paws, and they eat and kill all the animals and plants. What they like doing best is diving through the Sun. They can dive through a rainbow even. And one day they dived right through a rainbow and made a hole in it. All the colours began to drip out of the rainbow. I quickly turned myself into a fairy and flew up to the rainbow. They found me a very high stool with legs that stretched to the Earth and I knelt on it and coloured the rainbow all in again.

I'm glad I was able to do that because supposing the rainbow had been a Daddy rainbow which wanted to marry a Mummy rainbow and have a little girl rainbow. I think about that sometimes, and how cold they all must get when it snows.